POLLINATOR PALS

HANNAH THE HUMMINGBIRD POLLINATES

by Rebecca Donnelly
illustrated by Dean Gray

GRASSHOPPER

Tools for Parents & Teachers

Grasshopper Books enhance imagination and introduce the earliest readers to fiction with fun storylines and illustrations. The easy-to-read text supports early reading experiences with repetitive sentence patterns and sight words.

Before Reading

- Discuss the cover illustration. What do they see?
- Look at the glossary together. Discuss the words.

Read the Book

- Read the book to the child, or have him or her read independently.
- "Walk" through the book and look at the illustrations. Who is the main character? What is happening in the story?

After Reading

- Prompt the child to think more. Ask: Ruby-throated hummingbirds migrate when the seasons change. Can you think of any other animals that migrate?

Grasshopper Books are published by Jump!
5357 Penn Avenue South
Minneapolis, MN 55419
www.jumplibrary.com

Library of Congress Cataloging-in-Publication Data

Names: Donnelly, Rebecca, author.
Gray, Dean, illustrator.
Title: Hannah the hummingbird pollinates /
by Rebecca Donnelly; illustrated by Dean Gray.
Description: Minneapolis, MN: Jump!, Inc., [2022]
Series: Pollinator pals
Includes reading tips and supplementary back matter.
Audience: Ages 7-10.
Identifiers: LCCN 2021001281 (print)
LCCN 2021001282 (ebook)
ISBN 9781636902289 (hardcover)
ISBN 9781636902296 (paperback)
ISBN 9781636902302 (ebook)
Subjects: LCSH: Readers (Primary)
Ruby-throated hummingbird–Juvenile fiction.
Classification: LCC PE1119.2 .D6735 2022 (print)
LCC PE1119.2 (ebook)
DDC 428.6/2–dc23
LC record available at https://lccn.loc.gov/2021001281
LC ebook record available at https://lccn.loc.gov/2021001282

Editor: Eliza Leahy
Direction and Layout: Anna Peterson
Illustrator: Dean Gray

Printed in the United States of America at
Corporate Graphics in North Mankato, Minnesota.

Table of Contents

Finding Flowers

Hi, I'm Hannah! I'm a ruby-throated hummingbird. I don't have ruby-red feathers on my throat like this male. His bright colors help him attract a mate.

My feathers are good camouflage. They help me hide from predators!

I live in a city park. There are many tasty flowers here for me to drink from. Nectar is one of my favorite foods. It is sweet and tasty. I like nectar from red and orange flowers best.

I'm hungry! I move so fast, I need to eat all day long. I can visit more than one thousand flowers in a day! I also eat insects and spiders. They give me lots of energy.

Watch this! Did you know I'm the only bird that can fly backward? This helps me fly faster from flower to flower. My wings move so fast you can hardly see them! They beat 70 times a second. *Zip!*

wing

There's a honeysuckle!
My beak is long and thin.
Why? It helps me reach
into deep flowers like this!

honeysuckle

I might be tiny, but I can drink more than my weight in nectar every day. To drink, I hover in front of a flower.

I dip my beak in. Then I lap up the nectar with my tongue. Pollen gets on my beak and face.

Zip! I fly to another flower and drink some more. Some of the pollen on my beak and face rubs off onto the flower. This happens every time I land on a new flower. That's how I pollinate!

When I pollinate a flower, it grows seeds. The seeds grow into new plants.

Soon it will be fall. There won't be enough flowers for me to eat from. That means it's time for me to migrate. I will fly hundreds of miles to Central America. It's nice and warm there. Along the way, I will pollinate many more flowers. See you in spring!

Let's Review!

Hummingbirds pollinate many types of cone-shaped flowers with their long, thin beaks. Let's see how Hannah does it!

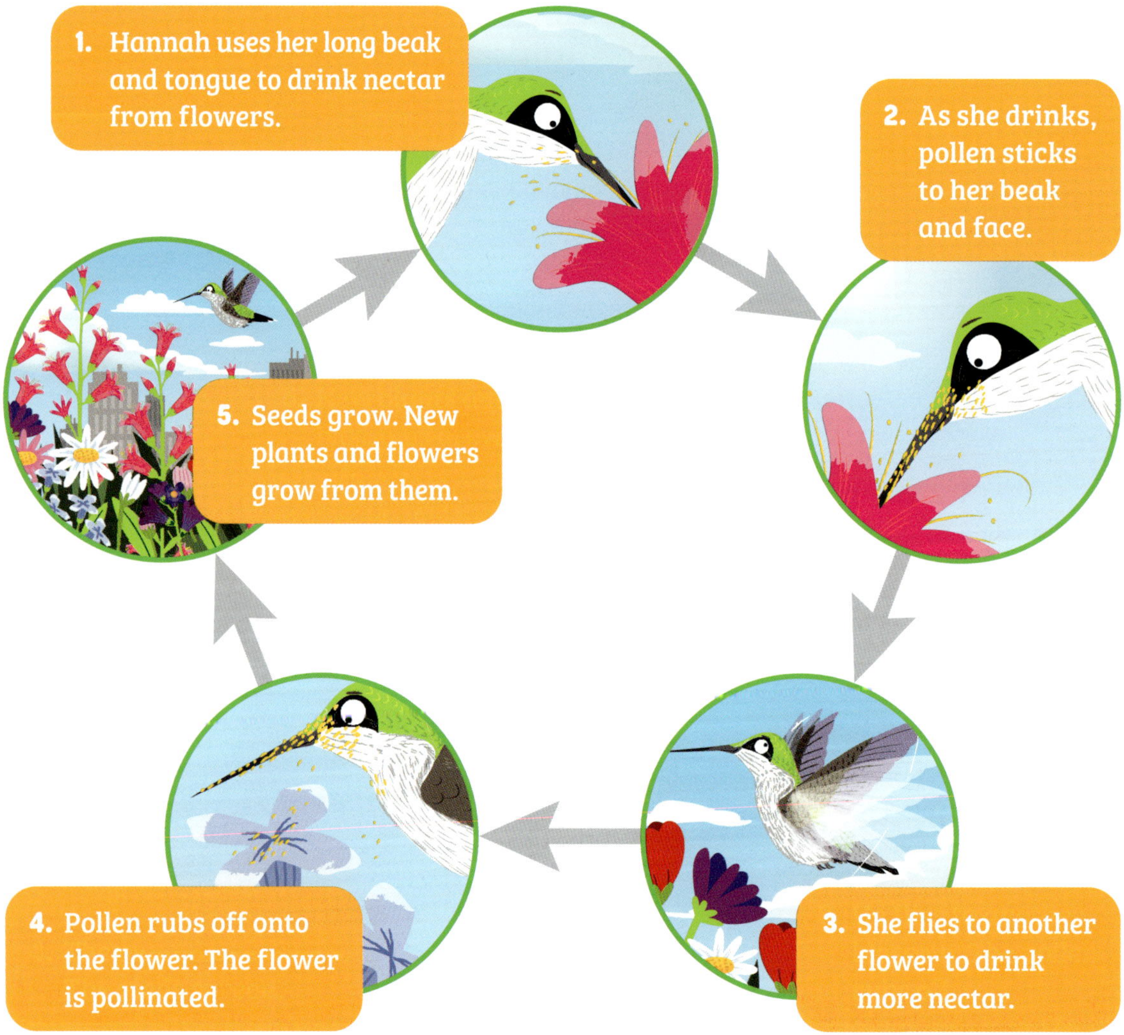

Where Ruby-Throated Hummingbirds Live

Hannah is a ruby-throated hummingbird. These hummingbirds live in Central and North America. Take a look!

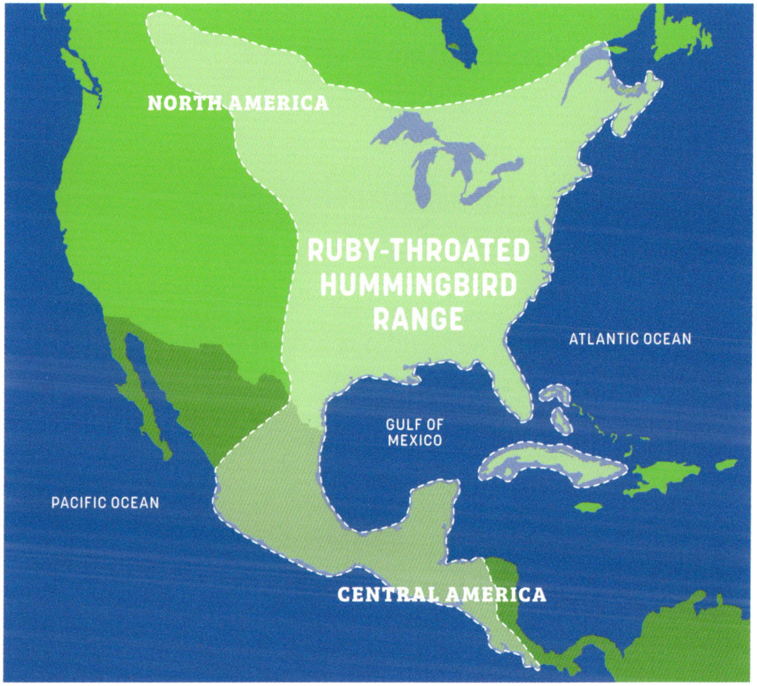

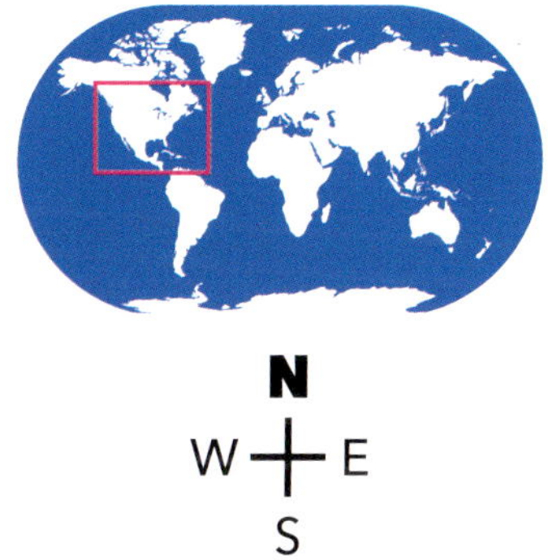

To Learn More

Finding more information is as easy as 1, 2, 3.

1. Go to www.factsurfer.com
2. Enter "**Hannahthehummingbirdpollinates**" into the search box.
3. Choose your book to see a list of websites.

Glossary

attract: To get one's interest.

camouflage: A disguise or natural coloring that allows animals to hide by making them look like their surroundings.

energy: The ability or strength to do things without getting tired.

hover: To remain in one place in the air.

mate: The male or female partner of a pair of animals.

migrate: To move to another area or climate at a particular time of year.

nectar: A sweet liquid made by flowers to attract pollinators.

pollen: A powder made by the male parts of plants.

pollinate: To take pollen from the male part of a flower and put it on the female part of a flower so the plant can reproduce.

predators: Animals that hunt other animals for food.

Index